For Marie and Jess
—P.M.

For my sister Louise
—S.B.

Text copyright © 2014 by Paula Metcalf
Jacket art and interior illustrations copyright © 2014 by Suzanne Barton

Visit us on the Web! randomhousekids.com

Educators and librarians, for a variety of teaching tools,
visit us at RHTeachersLibrarians.com

Library of Congress Cataloging-in-Publication Data
Metcalf, Paula.
A guide to sisters / by Paula Metcalf ; illustrated by Suzanne Barton. — First edition.
pages cm.
Summary: A big sister explains all there is to know about little sisters, divided into such categories as
Fun and Games, Style, and Sharing.
ISBN 978-0-553-49899-8 (trade)
[1. Sisters—Fiction.] I. Barton, Suzanne, illustrator. II. Title.
PZ7.M56568Gui 2016 [E]—dc23 2014014554

MANUFACTURED IN CHINA
10 9 8 7 6 5 4 3 2 1
First Edition

A Guide to Sisters

by Paula Metcalf
illustrated by Suzanne Barton

RANDOM HOUSE 🏠 NEW YORK

Contents

Introduction

If you're thinking about getting a sister
or you want to understand the one you
already have, this guide is for you.

1. Getting Started

Sisters come in two sizes: big

and little.

Most of the time, you get a new sister from the hospital. They are warm and squishy, like a freshly baked loaf of bread . . . but you should NOT put butter on them.

Also, they're a lot noisier.

"Waaahh!"

Sometimes you can *buy one, get one free.*

"WAAAAHH!"

Little sisters are very busy. They cry, eat, sleep, produce dirty diapers, and cry some more. But they DO give sweet baby kisses!

"AAAHH!"

And then their teeth come along. Teeny, adorable . . . sharp teeth.

"OUCH!"

2. On the Move

Another fun thing about little sisters is that they learn to walk! Then they can go every single place with their big sister (you).

(But keep a lookout for handy places to store them while you take care of important business.)

3. Cuteness

There is nothing as irresistible as a little sister! They are so cute that they have to get picked up, kissed, and whirled around many times each day. Luckily, big sisters don't have to go through all that.

4. A Gift

Mommies say, "A sister is the greatest gift a person can receive." (When they say this, they mean she's a gift for *you* . . . NOT that you should give her away at a birthday party!)

5. Fun and Games

Little sisters love pressing buttons. Their favorite button
is the one that switches the TV on and off,

on and off,

on and off, and

on and off.

"STOP THAT!"

Sometimes, big sisters wish little sisters
had an on-and-off button, too.
("Sigh.")

6. Tickling

This handy cutout shows the main ticklish spots of the little sister.

Little sisters can be wiggly, so for best results, have lots of pillows handy when tickling.

7. Style

Some have it . . .

. . . some don't.

Even though big sisters have to wait until their seventh birthday before they're allowed to wear high heels, little sisters only have to wait until their big sister's seventh birthday before *they're* allowed to wear high heels.

8. Clothes

If little sisters dress themselves,
it's best to check them over
before they leave the house.

"Your shoes are on the wrong feet!"
"No, they're not! These are MY feet!"

"Are you wearing pajamas under your tutu?"

9. Makeup

Big sisters are allowed to wear a little lip gloss and nail polish. Little sisters are not.

But who needs makeup when there are markers? LOTS of markers!

10. Sharing

Little sisters are really good at sharing.
They share your cakes, your cookies, your toys,
your clothes. . . .

Big sisters are really good at sharing, too.
"One for you, two for me . . ."

11. Making Stuff

Anything a little sister can do, a big sister can do better.

Big sisters can make a princess bed out of two cereal boxes,
four toilet-paper rolls, and an old towel.

Little sisters can make a princess toilet
out of the broken yogurt container
you didn't need for the princess bed.

Little sisters can also make two cereal boxes,
four toilet-paper rolls, and an old towel
out of a princess bed.

12. Cleaning Up

Big sisters! Try this:

Time your little sister to see how long she takes to pick up everything from your bedroom floor and put it where it belongs.

Track her progress, and see how happy she is
each week as she does it faster than the last time!

13. Bedtime

When night comes, it's time to put aside all the
day's fighting and be kind to each other.
"Would you like my doll tonight?"
"Hooray! Thank you!"

Now you can drift off to sleep happy that the person who knows you better than anyone else is right there.

Your friend, your bunk buddy, your partner, your secret keeper, your biggest fan, the greatest gift you can ever receive . . .

your sister!

P.S. Little sisters can sometimes get
scared in the middle of the night.
Big sisters can, too.